... But Noah found grace in the eyes of the Lord.

Other books by Peter Spier

NOAH'S ARK

NOAH'S ARK

Illustrated by Peter Spier

A ZEPHYR BOOK

Doubleday & Company, Inc., Garden City, New York

ISBN 0-385-17302-4 Paperbound   Illustrations and translation copyright © 1977 by Peter Spier

The Flood
Jacobus Revius (1586–1658)
Translated from the Dutch by Peter Spier

High and long,
Thick and strong,
Wide and stark,
Was the ark.
Climb on board,
Said the Lord.
Noah's kin
Clambered in.
Cow and moose,
Hare and goose,
Sheep and ox,
Bee and fox,
Stag and doe,
Elk and crow,
Lynx and bear,
All were there.
Stork and frog,
Skunk and hog,
Ape and snail,
Stoat and quail,

Flea and hound,
Could be found.
Lark and wren,
Hawk and hen,
Finch and kite,
Flew inside.
Dog and cat,
Mouse and rat,
Fly and vole,
Worm and mole,
Creatures all,
Large and small,
Good and mean,
Foul and clean,
Fierce and tame,
In they came,
Pair by pair,
Gross and fair.
All that walked,
Crawled or stalked

On dry earth
Found a berth.
But the rest,
Worst and best,
Stayed on shore,
Were no more.
That whole host
Gave the ghost.
They were killed
For the guilt
Which brought all
To the Fall.
Later on
It was done:
Back on land
Through God's hand,
Who forgave,
And did save.
The Lord's Grace
Be the praise!

... and he planted a vineyard.